This Orchard
book belongs to

_____

_____

_____

For my pesky little sisters,
Becky and Jess, with love.

ORCHARD BOOKS
338 Euston Road, London NW1 3BH
Orchard Books Australia
Level 17/207 Kent Street, Sydney, NSW 2000

First published in 2007 by Orchard Books
First published in paperback in 2008

Text and illustrations © Sam Lloyd 2007

The right of Sam Lloyd to be identified as the author and illustrator of
this work has been asserted by her in accordance with the Copyright, Designs
and Patents Act, 1988.

A CIP catalogue record for this book is available from the British Library.

ISBN 978 1 84616 523 8

3 5 7 9 10 8 6 4 2

Printed in China

Orchard Books is a division of Hachette Children's Books, an Hachette Livre UK Company.

Mr Pusskins
and Little Whiskers

Sam Lloyd

ORCHARD BOOKS

This is the story of a little girl called Emily, and her dear cat, Mr Pusskins.

Dum diddley dum dum, doo doo doo,
Sharing magic moments, just us two.

They thought life couldn't get any better.

Then, one day, Emily announced that she had a fabulous surprise for Mr Pusskins. He was **very** excited.

Emily fetched a large cardboard box, and inside the box was ...

...a kitten!

"This is Little Whiskers," said Emily. "She has come to live with us. She is only a tiny kitten, so we need to take care of her."

"I'm sure you two will be the best of friends," smiled Emily, "so I'll leave you to play lovely games together."

Mr Pusskins needed to be alone.
He was somewhat disappointed with his
'fabulous surprise', and he certainly
wasn't in the mood for 'lovely games'.

Little Whiskers wasn't in the mood
for **lovely games** either . . .

The pesky kitten took great delight in ruining all Mr Pusskins' special times.

She ruined telly time...

she ruined meal time...

she ruined play time...

she ruined nap time . . .

When Emily wasn't
looking, Little Whiskers ruined
EVERYTHING!

Mr Pusskins could bear it no longer.
Something had to be done.

So, that evening, Mr Pusskins wrote a letter.

To whom it may concern,

I am displeased with my 'fabulous surprise'. I find the kitten EXTREMELY irritating and wish to return her ASAP.

Yours fed-up-ingly,

Mr P

Tomorrow he would send it!

Then, Mr Pusskins settled down for a nice long sleep . . .

Suddenly, a hideous noise woke him. He dashed to see what was going on . . .

BAM BAM

CLUNK CLUNK

Emily dashed too. And who did she see?
"Mr Pusskins!" she gasped. "You know better
than to play such a terrible tune at this time
of night. You might have woken Little Whiskers!"

Emily banished Mr Pusskins outside.
"You need to think about what you've
done wrong," she said.

But Mr Pusskins hadn't done anything wrong. As rain turned to snow, he thought about his cosy home.

He reached up to the window to take
a peek . . . That wretched kitten! She was
already sitting in Mr Pusskins' favourite
spot by the fireside. Mr Pusskins was

FURIOUS!

But Little Whiskers wasn't enjoying the fireside. She knew **she** had been behaving naughtily, **not** Mr Pusskins.

How she wished there was a way she could make things better. And there was ...

Little Whiskers leapt onto the piano ...

BAM BAM
CLUNK CLUNK
BOOM BOOM BOOM BOOM

In rushed Emily. "Oh, good gracious!" she gasped. "Little Whiskers! It was **you** that played that terrible tune, wasn't it?!"

"Miaow," admitted the kitten.

Emily hurried outside. "My poor Mr Pusskins!
Please forgive me," she begged.
And, of course, Mr Pusskins did.

Little Whiskers
asked Mr Pusskins
to forgive her too.

And, eventually...

Mr Pusskins
DID!

Mr Pusskins didn't send the letter after all. He decided Little Whiskers could stay.

This is the end of the story of a little girl called Emily, and her dear cats, Mr Pusskins and Little Whiskers.

Dum diddley dum dum, dee dee dee,
Sharing magic moments, just us three!

And now,
life is perfect!